To my Fire Island family—The Prices, The Beermanns, The Humphreys, The Hortons,
Mary, TicTac, Rainbow and my beach bunny Samantha

For my mother, Leah,
And to my buddy Tom Slaughter, a fellow beach lover. —E.K.

with thanks for all our seashell days! —D.O.

Text copyright © 2015 by Dianne Ochiltree   Illustrations copyright © 2015 by Elliot Kreloff, All rights reserved/CIP data is available.

Published in the United States 2015 by ● Blue Apple Books, 515 Valley Street, Maplewood, NJ 07040 www.blueapplebooks.com

First Edition
Printed in China 05/15
ISBN: 978-1-60905-530-1
1 3 5 7 9 10 8 6 4 2

DIANNE OCHILTREE

It's a
Seashell
Day

illustrations by
ELLIOT KRELOFF

BLUE APPLE

When the sun peeks up over the bay,

Mommy tells me, "It's a seashell day!"

I rush down the path, over the dune.

Salty breeze blows. We'll be there soon!

We reach the beach.

Herring gulls flock.

Is this a seashell?

No. It's a rock!

With pail and shovel in my hand,

my toes squish in cool, wet sand.

A wave rolls in. It's way too big.
Go away, wave, so I can dig!

Bumpy, lumpy shells—
out from the muck.

Spiny, shiny shells—

a penny for luck!

My shell is tiny,
a silvery pearl.

Mommy's is brown
with a big, twirly curl.

"This shell is a home,"
Mommy tells me.
"Let's put it back
to live in the sea."

"This shell has a secret.
Hold it up to your ear."
"Listen," says Mommy.
"What do you hear?"

I count shells—

one, two, three, four.

Each one is different.

I have many more.

I count other shells—

five, six, seven, eight.

My shells are curvy—

never straight.

Two more shells—
numbers nine then ten.

When we get home,

Let's count them again.

We're almost home.

It's been a fun day.

So many shells—

I'll make a display!

One, two, three, four—a pretend seashell store.

Five, six, seven, eight—all my shells look really great!

WHELK SHELL

OYSTER SHELL

SCALLOP SHELL

MUSSEL SHELL

MOON SNAIL SHELL

Nine and ten—both from the sea.
I brought the beach home with me!

LIMPET
SHELL

CONCH SHELL

CONE SNAIL SHELL

RAZOR SHELL

CLAM SHELL

MY SHELLS

Mollusks are animals with soft bodies that wear their skeletons on the outside: seashells!

Seashells are mostly made of calcium. So are our bones!

Every empty seashell on the beach was once a part of an animal from the mollusk family.

There are more than 100,000 species of mollusks worldwide.

About half of all mollusks live in the ocean.

A seashell wraps around a mollusk's body like a suit of armor. It protects the sea creature living inside from predators and strong ocean currents undersea.

The best time to
find seashells on the beach
is in the morning or
evening at low tide.

Scallops have dozens of eyes
to help them see predators coming
from any direction.

Seashells can be
as small as a grain of rice
or as big as four feet across.

Hermit crabs
crawl into empty seashells
and call them home.
As hermit crabs grow bigger,
they have to find larger
and larger shells.

Many clams breathe
through a kind of 'snorkel', a body part
called a siphon, when they bury
themselves in sand.

Shells have been used
throughout history for art,
jewelry, money, tools,
containers and buttons.